SKULL OF ADAM

by
Stanley Moss

Horizon Press
New York, 1979

12/1979
am. lit.

ACKNOWLEDGMENTS

American Poetry Review: "Clouds," "Dog,"
"An Exchange of Hats," "Migrants"
American Review: "Apocrypha," "Shit," "Snot,"
"Vomit," "Potato Song," "On Seeing an X-Ray
of My Head"
Antaeus: "The Ice House"
Book Week: "Two Riders"
Encounter: "God Poem"
Michigan Quarterly Review: "Kangaroo," "Voice"
The Nation: "Che Guervara," "The Debt," "Love's
Edge," "Fact Song," "The Frog"
New American Review: "Poem Before Marriage"
The New Republic: "Fishermen I," "Fishermen II"
The New Yorker: "The Valley," "Old," "Clams"
Theater: "Prayer for Zero Mostel"
The Times Literary Supplement: "Before the Fire,"
"Clouds," "The Debt," "The Frog," "Goliath,"
"The Meeting," "On Seeing an X-Ray of My
Head," "Photography Isn't Art," "Potato Song,"
"Vomit"
Vanderbilt Poetry Review: "Jane's Grandmother"

The author gratefully acknowledges a supporting grant
from the Rockefeller Foundation.

The front cover shows Giovanni Bellini's *Pagan Allegory.*

for Jane

CONTENTS

1

2

3

4

1

On Seeing an X-Ray of My Head

This face without race or religion,
I have in common with humanity,
—mouth without lips, jaws without tongue,
this face does not sleep when I sleep,
gives no hint of love or pleasure,
my most recent portrait smells of fixative
and rancid vinegar, does not appear
male or female.
I don't look as if I work for a living.

I will ask for fire. I can't risk
lovers, walking in a wood, turn up this face,
see such putrefaction they question
why they've come to lie on the grass,
picnic, fish, or read to one another.
I will not have them find me staring
after their lovemaking,
—under the leaves and branches of summer,
a reminder of mortality.

I prefer the good life, in real death
a useful skull to house small fish
or strawberries, a little company.
I must remember death is not always
a humiliation, life everlasting
is to be loved at the moment of death.
I hold my lantern head before me,
peer into one eye, see darkness, darkness
in the other, great funerals of darkness
that never meet.

The Dog

I fly the flag of the menstruating black dog:
a black dog dripping blood over us all.
My flag barks, licks your face,
my flag says, "I am alive, willing,
part of the natural order of things.
You are a supernatural creature."

I walk across the road to the stream.
In a rush of water, — something surfaces,
— I hold my dog back.
A snake has caught a trout by the anus,
lifts the fish out of the water. The snake's head
cuts a line through the shaded stream
into the sunlight,
crosses the water to a ledge of gravel and jewelweed.
The trout is held into the summer air,
its brightest colors already begun to fade.
The snake uncoils and begins to devour the fish,
head first.

The trees remembering my mother
kiss me, because she told me:
be the sweet dog that licks the face and feet
of the bum passed out in the park,
—she caught a seed flying over a city street,
put it in her glove
took it home and planted it.
I sprawl with my dog on the floor
of all night restaurants
because the entire shape of time
is a greater, more ferocious beast
than anything in it.

Apocrypha

You lie in my arms,
sunlight fills the abandoned quarries.

I planted five Lombard poplars,
two apple trees died of my error,
three others should be doing better,
I prepared the soil,
I painted over the diseased apple tree,
I buried the available dead around it:
thirty trout that died in the pond
when I tried to kill the algae, a run-over raccoon,
a hive of maggots in every hole.
This year the tree flowered, bears fruit.
Are my cures temporary?

I chose abortion in place of a son,
because of considerations.

I look for the abandoned dead,
the victims, I shall wash them,
trim their fingernails and toenails.
I learn to say Kaddish,
to speak its Hebrew correctly,
a language I do not know,
should I be called upon.
I abandon flesh of my flesh
for a life of my choosing.

I take my life from Apocrypha.
Warning of the destruction of the city,
I send away the angel Raphael
and my son. Not knowing if I am right
or wrong, I fall asleep in the garden,
I am blinded by the droppings
of a hummingbird or crow.
Will my son wash my eyes with fish gall
restoring my sight?

You lie in my arms,
I wrestle with the angel.

Snot

I cannot forget the little swamp
that grows in my head,
cousin of the tear
snot, my lowly, not worthy of sorrow,
the body's only
completely unsexual secretion.
No one my dears is hot for snot
or its institutions: catarrh,
asthma, the common cold, although
I've heard "snot-nose" used to mean "darling"
or "my son." There's beauty in it,
familiar as the face of any friend.
Dogs eat it, no one gets rich on it.

Shit

I've been taught my daily lesson,
that man shall squat alone in secret,
I've been taken off my high horse,
I've bent down,
interrupted my day to humble myself,
no need to fall on my knees.
With a genuflection of the gut,
I hunt where my bones stink.

Let the mysterious ghost
of a turd pass between us,
— out of the pain of this world
a kindness, a shape each of us
learns by heart: moon crescent,
jewelweed, forget-me-not,
hot lava. Christ, is this
the ghost in everything,
what I can and cannot,
I will and will not,
I have and have not,
what I must and must not,
what I did and did not?
An infant gasps in ecstasy,
tears of shit drip from a man
who cannot cry.

Most men near death cannot withhold,
they shit on themselves,
when what they are
is all out of them:
wind, kindness, cruelty
all done, left behind,
when they must be changed,
and cannot remember
who chose to soil us,
who makes us clean.

Vomit

The stomach and the heart can be torn out
through the mouth if you get the right hook.
Because puking I was held up to this world,
because I have lived, burped in my mother's arms,
it comes out now:
what I thought I had swallowed, matters settled,
understood, kept out of mind, — our father
who keeps us in the speeding car,
who will not stop, let me puke in the grass
where it will hardly be noticed,
among the weeds and roadside flowers.

I throw up on myself the half-digested
meat and salad of what I devoured
in pleasure, the perfectly seasoned
explanation of love and social forces
that made me feel slightly superior.

I put my finger down my throat
so I can become part of this world,
I refuse to hear voices that speak to me
in rage without sense,
because my body and soul are locked
in secret battle, because the soul is voiceless
while the body can speak, gasp, sing, whisper,
utter what it pleases, because the body
becomes what it consumes and the soul

refuses such fires;
because the devil says
vomit is the speech of the soul.
I give the devil his due,
because the soul's speech is so rare,
to hear it
I must listen out of earshot,
I must give myself like a lover
and take like a lover, resisting and giving
till the heart is hooked and pulled out.

The Frog

I hold this living coldness,
this gland with eyes, mouth, feet,
shattered mirror of all creatures,
pulsing smile of fish, serpent and man,
just as I caught him most of my life ago
in the sawdust of the icehouse.

I could not believe in him if he was not here,
come from unwelcome phlegm
from black eggs strung through a swirl of water
settled in an unseen place.
A head that was also a tail broke out,
the first slight current taught his tail to swim.

Perhaps out of love of new sensation
or in a dream of being devoured,
by a thing part muskrat, part giant bass,
he moved into the shallowest water,
the sky and green branches above the stream
became familiar, feet grew out of him,
his tail fell off,
his lungs blew up with summer air.
The sound of his call is too large for his body:
"irrelevant, irrelevant, irrelevant."
Once in the dry countries he was a god.

Potato Song

Darkness, sunlight and a little holy spit
don't explain an onion with its rose windows
and presentiment of the sublime,
a green shoot growing out of rock,
or the endless farewells of trees.
Wild grasses don't grow just to feed sheep,
hold down the soil or keep stones from rolling,
they're meant to be seen, give joy, break the heart.
But potatoes hardly have a way of knowing.
They sense if it is raining or not,
how much sunlight or darkness they have,
not which wind is blowing or if there are crows
or red-winged blackbirds overhead.
They are almost unaware of the battles of worms,
the nightmares of moles, underground humpings.
Like soldiers in the field and the terribly poor,
they do not sleep or wonder. Sometimes
I hear them call me "mister" from the ditch.
Workers outside my window in Long Island
cut potatoes in pieces, bury them, water them.
Each part is likely to sprout and flower.
No one so lordly not to envy that.

Clams

Ancient of Days, bless the innocent
who can do nothing but cling,
open or close their stone mouths.
Out of water they live on themselves
and what little sea water they carry with them.
Bless all things unaware, that perceive
life and death as comfort or discomfort:
bless their great dumbness.

We die misinformed
with our mouths of shell open.
At the last moment, as our lives fall off,
a gull lifts us, drops us on the rocks, bare
because the tide is out. Flesh sifts the sludge.
At sea bottom, on the rocks below the wharf,
a salt foot, too humble to have a voice,
thumps for representation, joy.

2

Fishermen 1

My father made a synagogue of a boat.
I fish in ghettos, cast toward the lilypads,
strike rock and roil the unworried waters;
I in my father's image: rusty and off hinge,
the fishing box between us like a covenant.
I reel in, the old lure bangs against the boat.
As the sun shines I take his word for everything.
My father snarls his line, spends half an hour
unsnarling mine. Eel, sunfish and bullhead
are not for me. At seven I cut my name for bait.
The worm gnawed toward the mouth of my name.
"Why are the words for temple and school
the same," I asked, "And why a school of fish?"
My father does not answer. On a bad cast
my fish strikes, breaks water, takes the line.

Into a world of good and evil, I reel
a creature languished in the flood. I tear out
the lure, hooks cold. I catch myself,
two hooks through the hand,
blood on the floor of the synagogue. The wound
is purple, shows a mouth of white birds;
hook and gut dangle like a rosary,
another religion in my hand.

I'm ashamed of this image of crucifixion.
A Jew's image is a reading man.
My father tears out the hooks, returns to his book,
a nineteenth-century history of France.
Our war is over:
death hooks the corner of his lips.
The wrong angel takes over the lesson.

Fishermen 2

In late September on a school day
I take my father, failing, now past seventy
to the row boat on the reservoir, the waters
since July have gone down two hundred yards
below the shoreline.
The lake stretches before us — a secret,
we do not disturb a drifting branch, a single hawk.
For a moment nothing says, "thou shalt not."
If I could say anything to the sky and trees
I'd say things are best as they are.

It is more difficult for me to think
of my father's death than my own.
He casts half the distance he used to.
I am trying to give him something,
to stuff a hill between his lips. I try
to spoon feed him nature, but an hour
in the evening on the lake does not nourish him,
the walk in the woods that comforts me
as it used to comfort him, makes him shiver.
I pretend to be cold.

We walk back along the old lake bottom,
our shoes sink into the cold mud —
where last spring there was ten foot of water,
where last summer I saw golden carp
coupling on the surface. It's after dark,
although I can barely see
I think I know where the fence is.

My father's hands tremble like the tail of a fish
resting in one place. As for me?
I have already become his ghost.

Old

The turtles are out,
loners on the road listening for mud,
old people looking for money.
Father, too old for hope,
when trees are burned black with cold,
what belongs to man, and what to nature?

A shell of your old self,
once you took a penknife,
scraping out the living flesh,
made an ashtray of a turtle,
mine to take home if I want it.
I want to whisper
the prayers and psalms you never taught me.
I never learned a healthy disrespect,
to render unto Caesar or to God.
On my table I keep a bronze turtle
—a handle torn from an African sword,
a symbol of destroyed power.

The turtles move under the snow
in the dead of winter, under the loam,
chewing and scratching into frozen sand,
deeper than hiding grubs or hunting moles,
far from the loneliness of sunlight and weather.
I offer my hand, a strange other element.

in my apartment, like last summer,
I have only to touch the thermostat,
the air cools and fans.
What was that? A light turns on and off
at a distance, as if someone crossed
between me and fire, — or was signaling.
Possibly the wind bent a branch across
a lighted window, or an automobile
turned away.
Her passion was almost unnoticeable,
— like the statue of Saint Teresa in ecstasy,
looking to heaven, a single toe crooked sharply,
her mouth barely open, showing the edge
of a marble tongue. How was I to know?
Flesh is a ghost, inarticulate.

Squall

I have not used my darkness well,
nor the Baroque arm that hangs from my shoulder,
nor the Baroque arm of my chair.
The rain moves out in a dark schedule.
Let the wind marry. I know the creation
continues through love. The rain's a wife.
I cannot sleep or lie awake. Looking
at the dead I turn back, fling
my hat into their grandstands for relief.
How goes a life? Something like the ocean
building dead coral.

The Return

It was justice to see her nude haunches
backing toward me again after the years,
familiar as water after long thirst.
Now like a stream she is, and I can lie beside
running my hand over the waters, or sleep,
— but the water is colder, the gullies darker,
the rapids that threw me down have shallowed,
— I can walk across.

Prayer

Give me a death like Buddha's. Let me fall
over from eating mushrooms Provençal,
a peasant wine pouring down my shirt-front,
my last request not a cry but a grunt.
Kicking my heels to heaven, may I succumb
tumbling into a rose bush after a love
half my age, — though I'm deposed, my tomb
shall not be empty, may my belly show above
my coffin like a distant hill, my mourners come
as if to pass an hour in the country,
to see the green, that old anarchy.

Poem Before Marriage

I am part man, part sea gull, part turtle.
What remains? I have a few seasons
of vanity and forty years in the muddy lake.
I float on the reservoir in Central Park,
my gull eyes, man flesh, turtle mouth, tear the water
hunting shadows of fish that never appear.
I live on things a great city
puts in a small bowl for emergencies.
I "Caw Caw," wishing the shell on my back
were a musical instrument.
I have already been picked out of the mud
three times, and thrown
against apartment house walls, left for dead.
I am a snapper, a mean-looking bastard.

Jane, in my bed you will find feathers
and fragments of shell, — when, swallowing
    darkness,
I have a nightmare in your arms, my eyes
film over, let me sink to the bottom
of the artificial lake.

Fish for me.

Song

Why do you pick only the smallest wild flowers?
The daisy and day lily aren't gross,
lilacs, peonies and roses
aren't base company.
Why are they so small, the wild flowers
you bring me,
the most delicate, purest of color?
What is their purpose,
brought by your hand to the hand of your lover?

The Valley

Once I was jealous of lovers.
Now I am jealous of things that outlast us
— the road between Route 28 and our house,
the bridge over the river,
a valley of second growth trees.
Under the birches, vines
the color of wolves, survive a winter ten below,
while the unpicked apples turn black
and the picked fruit is red in the basket.
I am not sure that the hand of God
and the hand of man ever touch,
even by chance.

3

God Poem

Especially he loves
his space and the parochial darkness.
They are his family, from them grow his kind:
idols with many arms and suns that fathered
the earth, among his many mirrors, and some
that do not break:
rain kept sacred by faithful summer grasses,
fat Buddha and lean Christ, bull and ram,
horns thrusting up his temple and cathedral,
— mirrors, but he is beyond such vanities.
Easy to outlive
the moment's death having him on your knees,
— grunting and warm he prefers wild positions:
he mouths the moon and sun, brings his body
into insects that receive him beneath stone,
into fish that leap as he chases,
or silent stones that receive his silence.
Chivalrous and polite the dead take
his caress, and the sea rolling under him
takes his fish as payment and his heaps of shells.

II

As he will,
he throws the wind arch-backed on the highway,
lures the cat into moonlit alleys,
mountains and fields with wild strawberries.
He is animal,
his tail drags uncomfortably, he trifles
with the suck of bees and lovers, so simple
with commonplace tongues, — his eyes ripple
melancholy iron and carefree tin,
his thighs are raw from rubbing, cruel as pine,
he can wing an eagle off a hare's spine,
crouch with the Sphinx, push bishops down
in chilly chapels, a wafer in their mouths,
old men cry out his passage through their bowels.

III

No word, none of these, no name, "Red Worm!
     Snake!"
What name makes him leave his hiding place?
Out of the null and void,

no name and no meaning: God, Jahweh, the Lord,
not to be spoken to, he never said a word
or took the power of death: the inconspicuous
plunge from air into sea he gave to us,
winds that wear away our towns...Who breathes
comes to nothing: absence, a world.

An Exchange of Hats

I will my collection of hats,
straw the Yucatan, fez Algiers 1935,
Russian beaver, Irish fisherman's knit,
collapsible silk opera, a Borsalino,
to a dead man,
the Portuguese poet, my dear Fernando,
who without common loyalty,
wrote under seven different names
in seven different styles.
He was a man of many cafes,
a smoker and non smoker.
His poets, come to live in Lisbon,
had different sexual preferences,
histories and regional accents.

Still their poems had a common smell
and loneliness that was Fernando's.
His own character
was to him like ink to a squid,
something to hide behind.
What did it matter, writing in Portuguese
after the first World War? The center was Paris,
the languages French and English.

In Lisbon, workers on the street corner were arguing
over what was elegance, the anarchist manifesto,
the trial of Captain Artur Carlos De Barros,
found guilty of "advocating circumcision"
and teaching Marranos no longer to enter church
saying "When I enter I adore neither wood nor stone
but only the Ancient of Days who rules all."
The Portuguese say
they have the "illusion" to do something,
meaning they very much want to do it.

He could not just sit in the same cafe
wearing his own last hat, drinking port
and smoking *Ideals* forever.

Sign

My friends, Moss is on the fence in Long Island,
the sea a distance away like a grandfather
at a family reunion, says it's all sand.
But Moss is on the fence, — it might as well
be charged with high voltage, or painted blue
for all the good that will come of that.
It is a fact and if I scrape my name off
with a knife, the wood is wet underneath,
just as sand is moist when you kick it up.
I suppose something like this wetness and the sun
made the first living thing, the first sub-roach
that danced its way from under dead matter.
In the beginning before darkness was there a death?

Of course the wind or a telephone call
moves the earth a little, — damn little,
the apple falls like an apple, and leaves
hit the deck in their leafy way, and Moss
shall be no exception. One fine day
shall I come down like some heavy vine?
More likely a mange of lungs
contracted from the beginning
in the wetness, in the sun.
Any day is a good day to be born,
any day is a good day to die.
Days learn from the day,
nights to the night show knowledge.

SM

With spray can paint,
I illuminate my name
on the subway cars and hand ball courts,
in the public school yards of New York,
S M
written in sky-above-the-ocean blue,
surrounded by a valentine splash
of red and white, not for Spiritus Mundi,
but for a life and death, part al fresco
part catacomb,
against the city fathers
who have made a crime of signaling
with paint to passengers and pedestrians.
For the ghetto population of my city
I spray my name
with those who stand for a public art
that doesn't disillusion our sacred lives.
In secret if I must
and wearing sneakers, I sign with those
who have signed for me.

Two Riders

I am death's Sancho Panza.
"What is my Lord like," you ask,
"is he kind, is he clean?"
He likes to watch a ship in high seas,
lifted almost out of the water,
and the crash of the ship sounding.
He will not listen to Saint Jude,
patron of lost causes and incurables.
When some men die, their beds,
tables and chairs fly out with them.
I ride a length behind.
I know how to make do.
Even in hell
a hundred years from now,
I'll teach English or sell.
You can always find
a little sanguine drawing
of paradise in hell.

Migrants

I

Foggy weather.
The most aloof birds
come closer to the earth,
confused by the apparent
lowering of the clouds and sky.
I walk in these descended clouds,
set birds off in terror.
The fish don't care.
I surf cast a silver spoon
into the clouds
in the direction of the sea.

II

Last summer in Long Island
I saw a pair of white egrets
standing at the shoreline.
Now I see hundreds of them
swooping above me,
more delicate than gulls—
beyond Fern Gully
where the road leads into fields of sugar cane,
the old slave plantations.

The flights of white birds
remind me of alarmed swallows.
Then I see what they are doing:
hundreds of birds are driving
a single buzzard out of the valley.
I am afraid of what I see.
I suppose they are diving again and again
to protect their nests.
In just a few days
I have become accustomed
to seeing egrets perched on cattle
or standing silently beside
in apparent repose.
Now I see them fighting for life,
summoning whatever violence they have,
unable to be graceless.
One by one, not as a flock,
the birds dive, pursue,
but do not touch.
Off the Caribbean,
a fresh afternoon wind
lifts the egrets higher
and gives the red-throated scavenger,
who must also feed its young,
a momentary passage
down into the tall, moist grass.

Jamaica, W.I.

Fact Song

1

Benjamin Franklin, late in his 84th year,
his last year,
on a voyage across the Atlantic,
kept throwing out a bottle on a string,
pulled it up, then threw it out again,
He arrived in New York,
tossed his hat from ship to shore,
having just proved
the existence of the Gulf Stream.

2

Ancient Hebrew judges
listed the crimes
for which the penalty of death
might be given, but added
woe be unto any judge
who had given the sentence
more than once in seven years,
and any court in which the death penalty
had been pronounced
should be known from then on
as the court of the assassins.

3

Obscure orders of monks and nuns
make the Seder, observing
most Christians base their holiest sacrament
on something Christ said when he celebrated
the Passover meal,
"This is my body, this is my blood,"
the promise of everlasting life,
— ignoring the other lesson
that he was himself spending the evening
celebrating the escape of the Jews from Egypt,
drinking to the everlasting life of a people
as a people.

4

It is good to keep the future holy,
I know more of what isn't than what is.
If working in your garden,
they run to you saying the Messiah is coming,
first plant another tree
then go to meet the Messiah.

Goliath

I am part man, part snake,
I lie in your lap like a book,
I can tell a tale of base and divine crevices,
of wordless places, unreachable ledges,
high waterfalls, clouds, dropping down
to swamp lands.
I lingered on the footpaths in gardens
of oleanders and lemon trees,
but my flesh was torn and I tore flesh.
Solo I dangled, whimpered, wept, begged.
I have fathered and mothered, poisoned the nipple,
I offered fruit I would never eat.
I slipped into the furthest valley,
places without ornament:
deserted barracks.
I commanded a territory. I am Goliath,
a child has flung a stone into my head.

Voice

My voice has been imprisoned
in the voice of a crowd in a stadium,
before the grandstands empty
leaving behind my voice among the stragglers,
in idle conversation, in the odd shout.

I wanted to have a river to work with,
a voice that thirsts and drinks,
swimming and diving among the nude bathers,
surrounding the body it chooses.

I did not want my voice to be only a difference
of shadow as a black pine is in the night.
I wanted my voice to be a different, moon-like thing
that those on foot can see by.
I wanted my voice to reappear
suddenly in the night,
to last after touch, taste, sight, hearing

4

Photography Isn't Art

1

If I gave up the camera
or really made myself into a camera
or into a photograph,
if the sight of that photograph
made me change my life,
if I really held my darkest self
up to the light,
where life cannot be violated
by enlargers, light meters,
— what creature would such changes keep alive?

My work changes color because of the work
like the hands of people handling coins.
The pregnant black woman
I saw during the blackout in New York City
carrying a refrigerator on her back,
was not only a likeness.
Visions hide more than they reveal.

2

If I could really become a blur,
if I became for the joy of it — say a photograph
taken in a forgiving light,
of the guests seated around the table
at Delacroix's dinner party Paris, 1857,
when he had just made an omelette
so beautiful no one would eat it,
then if they called me to join at table
that company of poets and painters,
I would sweep the skull of Adam off the cloth,
smile for the photographer,
give thanks and suggest
we eat the omelette while it is still hot.

Lovers

We are gravel in the river bed.
Years set us together in a bed of clay.
The river passes over us like suffering,
spring rains wash out the pine saplings,
in loneliness great trees sweep downstream,
— avalanche, falling shale, water becomes mud,
becomes rock, willows root, startled trout
rest and spawn upon us,
a fisherman may push his boot
into our throats.

We know there are mountains:
we see them above the waters
as a single purple, blue and white blossom.
The river has changed course, leaving its bed.
What can I bring you,
facing the moon and the mountain?
We are used to seeing the water,
then the moonlight on the surface of the water,
then the night, finally the moon itself.
The world comes, offers bread and fish
not stone and serpent.

Morning

Usually I wake
to a dreamlike landscape,
face outside my window
—the Atlantic, a Catskill stream,
or the lake in Central Park.
My breath stares,
my tongue regards,
I whisper in my wife's ear,
"Are you up?"
Some voices can see,
some voices see for others, change the world.
All my voice can do is sleep near her ear,
while she chooses to sleep or wake.

Jane's Grandmother

Light as a sparrow
she sits on a burnished leather Davenport,
the kind you can't slump in.
Near her 104th year, her death is almost lost
like the comb that keeps her hair in place,
her vanity long since cut down like poplars:
useless soft wood.
I know rivers younger than she is.
She wears a charred black shawl of burned houses
built again, sold, and burned again,
and wild flowers of the Rockies.
In Montana the clouds are younger than she is,
— there's not much standing between anything
    and the sky, —
the darkness older,
some trees older, the great withstanders.
The barbed wire runs from U.S. 6
into her fingers and arms.
The last breath and the first are as holy,
for all the lips
the breath has passed over,
— old breath bruising with breathlessness.
Matter of fact: you can ask her mercy,
the poor come and get more
than broken stars and blue firmament.
Her daughters care for her fingernails,
brown shell of box turtle.
They wash the clam gray under her arms.

Bless her for her whisky sours, and hating Nixon.
Suddenly out of the bushes
a wild turkey in the moonlight.
Her smile moves to the rings of a tree,
her daughters' faces and their daughters'.

Che Guevara

Anyone can see suffering
made him look like Christ,
tied on a donkey,
fainting like a girl,
an icon on the front page
of the New York Times,
somebody's dead lover.

Prayer For Zero Mostel (1915-1977)

Señor, already someone else,
O my clown,
the man in your image
was a bestiary,
sweet as sugar,
beautiful as the world,
lizard sitting on a trellis
follows blonde into john,
now a butterfly on the edge
of a black-eyed susan,
rhinoceros
filing down his own horn
for aphrodisiac.
Señor, already someone else,
a band of actors under bombardment
played Shakespeare,
the last few days
of the Warsaw ghetto,
a few of the survivors
who crawled through the sewers
heard the SS was giving out visas
for America
at a certain hotel,
went to apply.

If you love life
you simply can't believe
how bad it is.
Señor, someone else,
a Jahweh clown,
rectal thermometer of the world,
the tears themselves leave scars.
Farewell art of illusion,
playing yourself as a crowd.

Nicky

She danced into the moonless winter,
a black dog.
In the morning when I found her
I couldn't get her tongue back in her mouth.
She lies between a Japanese maple
and the cellar door, at no one's feet,
without a master.

Two Minutes Early

1

You say I read clocks like a Roman
reading chicken guts for omens.
Something sacred may happen.
Waiting, I can't tell time.
The woodpile is a clock,
dead hours and weeks
cut and stacked,
left to dry out and weather,
till the last green minute
burns without hissing.
At the crotch of a tree,
a beehive is a clock,
minutes and seconds swarming
over each other,
till a fat second stings me.
The sweetest honey
isn't made of clover
but of wild thyme
and its blue flower.

2

The years are silent as waterlilies,
buggy, turning brown.
Two minutes, — in such an interval,
in such a cocoon,
in this darkness of tiny skies
illuminated by moons
or blown into nights,
held up by a twig, —
a tough little worm works
on the edge of a leaf,
unfolds a single black wing
that parts a moment later
showing two yellow and black wings.
What part of the sun and moon are you?

3

My tongue leads me to the darkest darkness
near the light, beside you.
It seems whatever time of the day it seems,
the sky doesn't sort out what's storming now
from ancient tempest, from what's to come.
I'm grateful for the time of day.
A summer rain takes over my life,
then simply abandons me.

Clouds

Working class clouds are living together
above the potato fields, — tall white beauties
humping above the trees, burying their faces
in each other, — clouds with darker thighs,
rolling across the Atlantic. West,
a foolish cumulus hides near the ocean
afraid of hurricanos.
Zeus came to the bed
of naked Io, as a cloud,
passed over her and into her as a cloud,
all cloud but part of his face
and a heavy paw, half cloud, half cat
that held her down.
I take clouds to bed that hold me
like snow and rain, gentle ladies,
wet and ready, smelling of lilac hedges.
I swear to follow them like geese,
through factory smoke,
beyond the shipping lanes and jet routes.
They pretend nothing — opening, drifting, naked.
I pretend to be a mountain
because I think clouds like that.
A cloudy night
proclaims a condition of joy.
Perhaps I remember a certain cloud,
perhaps I bear a certain allegiance
to a certain cloud.

Before the Fire

My face leans to touch
things fallen through blades of grass,
things too small to pick up between my fingers:
fleck of stem, edge of husk,
fragments of petal and old grass.
I lean on one hand.
They come up sticking to my palm,
— my brothers and sisters of no consequence.

Under the loneliness of smoke,
I cross out such lines as
"...no wind can turn the fire
from dry grass,
from king maple or scrub oak,"
— because any wind can turn fire a little.

Beside the non-existing,
every grub is an elephant
with arms of sunlight and prayer,
every leaf a mandarin
accountable to an ancient dynasty.
A branch of white pine two yards long,
still green with sap and privilege,
represents the last joy in the fire.

The Meeting

It took me some seconds as I drove toward
the white pillow case, or was it a towel
blowing across the road, to see what it was.
In Long Island near the sanctuaries
where there are still geese and swan,
I thought a swan was hit by an automobile.
I was afraid to hurt it. The beautiful creature
rolled in sensual agony,
then reached out to attack me.
Why do I feel something happened on the road,
a transfiguration, a transgression,
as if I hadn't come to see what was,
but confronted the white body,
tried to lift, help her fly,
or slit its throat.
Why did I need this illusion,
a beauty lying helpless?

The Debt

I owe a debt to the night,
I must pay it back, darkness for darkness
plus interest.
I must make something out of almost nothing,
I can't pay back by just not sleeping
night after night. I hear them screaming
in the streets of New York, "What? What? What?"

I can't write a check to the night,
or a promissory note: "I'll write songs."
Only the nightmare is legal tender.
I bribe owls, I appeal
to creatures of the night: "Help me
raccoons, catfish, snakes!"
I put my head in the tunnel of a raccoon,
pick up a fish spine in my mouth.
Perhaps the night will accept this?
Dying is my only asset.

These days driving along I turn up my brights.
I love and am grateful for anything that lights
the darkness: matches, fireworks, fireflies.
My friend who's been to Antarctica
tells me against the ice when the sun is high
you see the shadow of the earth.
The night after all is just a shadow...
The debt keeps mounting.

I try to repay something by remembering
my Dante, the old five and ten thousand lira notes
had Dante's face etched on the front.
(I bought that cheap). Hard cash to the night
is finding out what I do not want to know
about myself, no facts acceptable,
— a passage through darkness,
where one I stop to ask, "Why? What?"
is always myself, I cannot recognize.

If only I could coin nightmares:
— a barnyard in Asia,
the last dog and cat betrayed, are no more.
A small herd of three-legged blind cows
still gives milk.
A pig with a missing snout, its face like a moon,
wades in a brook.
A horse, its mane burnt to cinders,
a rear hip socket shot off, tries to get up
thrusting its muzzle into the dark grass.
A rooster pecks without a beak or a coxcomb.
A rabbit that eats stones, sips without a tongue,
runs without feet.
A ditch of goats, sheep and oxen
locked in some kind of embrace.
All move their faces away,
refuse the charity of man
the warrior, the domesticator.

I see a whale with eyes yards apart
swimming out of the horizon,
surfacing as if it were going to die,
with a last disassociated vision,
one eye at peace
peers down into the valleys and mountains
of the ocean, the other eye floats,
tries to talk with its lids to the multitude.
While in the great head
what is happening and what happened mingle,
for neither has to be.
I pray for some of my eyes to open
and some to close.
It is the night itself that provides
a forgiveness.

Kangaroo

My soul climbs up my legs,
buries its face in blood and veins,
locks its jaws on the nipple that is me,
I jump my way into the desert.
What does my soul, safe in its pocket care
what I say to desert flowers?
Like a kangaroo
I pray and mock prayer.

I never took a vow of darkness.
I sit beside a boulder writing
on yellow lined paper. Once I thought
— I'll pull my soul out of my mouth,
a lion will sleep at my feet,
I'll spend forty days in the desert,
I'll find something remarkable, a sign:
strains of desert grass
send the root of a single blade
down thirty feet,
I remember flakes of dry blood,
the incredible rescue of the man by the soul.

Under the aching knuckles of the wind,
move down in your pocket
away from remorse and money.
learn discomfort from the frog,
the worm, the gliding crow,
they all hunt in repose, like men in prayer.

I can hardly distinguish myself from darkness.
I am not what I am. I demand the heart
to answer for what is given. I jump into the desert,
a big Jew, the law under my arm like bread.

The Branch

Since they were morose in August,
not worth saving,
I paid to have the junipers torn out
trunk and root, the roots had enough strength
to pull the truck back down so hard
the wheels broke the brick walk.

Heaped in front of my house,
cousins of the tree of mercy,
the green and dry gray branches
that did not suffer
but had beauty to lose.
Damp roots, what do I know
of the tenderness of earth,
the girlish blond dust?
Rather than have the branches dumped or burned
I dragged them to the bulkhead
and pushed them into the sea.

I know the story of a tree:
of Adam's skull at the foot of Jesus crucified,
of the cross made of timbers nailed together
that Roman soldiers saved from the destroyed
    temple,
that King Solomon built from a great tree
that rooted and flourished
from a branch of the tree of mercy

planted in dead Adam's mouth,
that the branch was given
to Adam's third son Seth by an angel
that stopped him outside the wall
when he returned to the garden,
that the angel warned him
that he could not save his father
who was old and ill
with oils or tears or prayers.

Go in darkness, mouth to mouth
is the command.
I kiss the book,
not wanting to speak
of the suffering I have caused.
Sacred and defiled,
my soul is right
to deal with me in secret.